ISBN: 9798862432787

Self-Published, 2024

Cover illustration designed and Created by Kay Baldock.

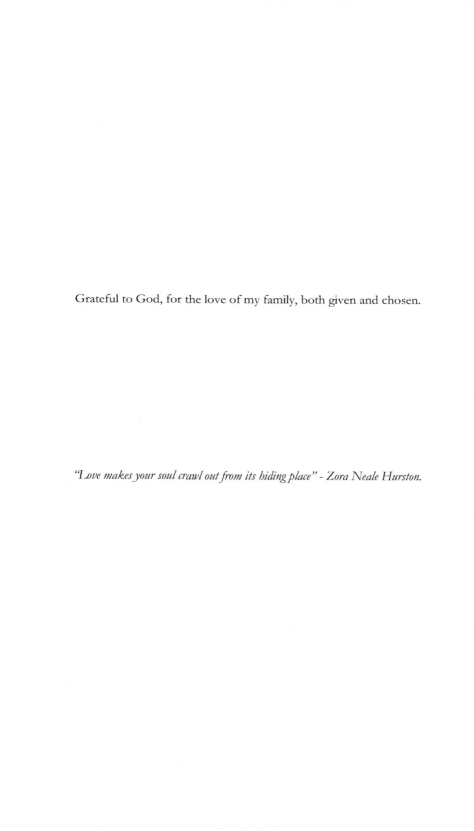

Grateful to God, for the love of my family, both given and chosen.

"Love makes your soul crawl out from its hiding place" - Zora Neale Hurston.

The Prelude of Longing.

1.

Unsung ardor whispers

to the hollows of a vacant room,

A melody only the wind dares carry.

through the silent gloom.

It lingers in the split-second before sleep claims,

Lips parting for a kiss that remains a dream,

In the quiet, my heart composes odes,

For an orchestra led only by the moon's soft beams.

2.

Amid the gentle hush of twilight, under a sky blushing with stars,

Two sets of eyes meet, casting a silent spell in the evening's quietude.

No words spoken, yet volumes conveyed through that lingering look.

Untouched remains the world around, as burgeoning hearts pulse,

Echoing with the potent whispers of possibility,

Chasing the tantalizing allure of "What might be?".

3.

In the soft tangle of linen,

A hollow where you are meant to lie,

Shadows play in the absence of light,

While morning stretches, quiet and shy.

Where whispers should tangle in the dark,

Only silence meets the day's start,

And in the breadth where dreams are spun,

I trace the outlines of a missing part.

Awaiting the weight of shared dreams and sighs,

Each dawn is anticipation's silent crescendo,

As I mark the place for you,

In the bed where love is meant to echo.

4.

Under the vast canopy of stars,

I rehearse silent conversations with you,

Choreographing a duet

The universe has yet to score.

5.

The park bench, aglow with the fading light of day, cradles a multitude of untold tales,

A silent witness to the tender encounters that unfold at the cusp of evening.

Each couple's gaze weaves a tapestry of near misses and quiet hopes,

Their eyes painting portraits of yearning in the amber hue of twilight.

Almost-touches linger in the space between fingers,

A ballet of hesitant movements choreographed by the pulse of hearts in wait.

The bench holds the imprint of budding romance,

A sanctuary for whispered promises and laughter that hangs in the cooling air.

In the quiet moments as the sun dips low,

This unassuming perch becomes a vessel of potential,

Cupping the delicate beginnings of affection yet to bloom,

Of love's sweet prologue, poised to be written beneath the watchful sky.

6.

The throb of a heart alone,

Beats a solitary rhythm against thick silence,

a rhythm once lively, now dulled,

by the solitude that envelops its cadence.

Crooning for a duet, harmonies incomplete,

It sways in the chamber of the unfulfilled.

Echoes of laughs, echoes of steps,

Each a phantom, in the heart's theatre still.

7.

Canvas unmarred by love's colours,

Yearns for the brush's tender stroke.

My soul awaits its masterpiece —

The touch of an unseen artist.

8.

Night whispers secrets of lovers' past,

Dreams filter through the sieve of reality,

Love, a fleeting shade, eludes me,

In the gardens of the night.

9.

The moon casts its longing gaze across the vastness,

A silent admirer of the ocean's ceaseless grace.

Its luminescent touch caresses the waves,

In a nightly courtship too vast for embrace.

This celestial dance of distant paramours,

Unfolds in the hushed ballet of the night.

Their union told in the gentle pull of tides,

And the sea's murmured replies to the moon's soft light.

Together, they whisper the oldest of love tales,

A romance written in the ebb and flow of time.

In their wordless yearning, a mirror for lovers,

Each glance, each ripple, a testament sublime.

10.

The library of my yearning heart,

heavy with volumes of unwritten affection,

Awaits the penning of our narrative,

Each page anticipating your gentle inflection.

Words wrapped in future tense, a tale untold,

Shelved among the 'yet to be,' and 'might'—

The unfinished stories seek authorship,

In your hands, the potential to alight.

11.

Amidst the ceaseless thrum of city's tide,

I stand as but a vessel for our tale untold.

My heart, an open chamber set wide,

Awaits your script in letters bold.

In every passing smile that strangers share,

Potential lines of our story wait to unfold.

Could fate pen us together without delay?

As life resumes where once it hesitated, cold.

Through bustling avenues, we move unseen,

Our narrative dormant 'til you step from crowd's veil.

With each encounter, what might have been

Is etched upon the moment, delicate and frail.

Yet hope persists beyond the urban roar—

An act awaits with you I've yet to explore.

12.

Echoes of future laughter linger

In the rooms where shadows dance alone,

A prelude to the symphony,

I've yet to compose with you.

13.

In silence shared, a texture rich, unspun,

A fabric waiting warmth from you alone.

Loose threads dangle, waiting to be one,

On loom of hope where threads of trust are sown.

The quiet holds a space for us to fill,

A space bare, where whispered dreams might dance.

Awaiting still, the weaver's tender skill,

To join these threads in fate's intricacies.

14.

The scent of seasons shifting on the wind,

Bears subtle hints of you in its embrace.

Each fallen petal stands as quiet guard,

A testament to solitude's own grace.

These sentinels to days spent all alone,

Beneath a sky where distant stars convene.

Await the one whose essence feels like home,

To join and savor love's yet tasted scene.

15.

Twilight drapes its veil, a quiet interlude,

Where light and shadow softly coalesce.

The heart, in this half-light, feels more acutely,

The solitude that day does not confess.

Dusk's gentle hymn, a melody of nearness,

Suggests a presence just beyond the veil,

A dance of hope and longing in the gloaming,

A silent wish that twilight might unveil.

16.

Autumn's breath, in playful swirls, does tease

The amber leaves, a mimic of your mirth—

A laughter still unknown to ear,

Yet missed, as if it warmed my days on earth.

17.

In the quiet, I fashion daydreams

Of you, like origami hopes,

Folding corners of reality

Into a delicate wish.

18.

Yearning stretches like the shore's sand,

Eager for the sea's caress —

I am the land, bound and waiting,

For the tide that is your presence.

19.

Unpenned sonnets lay dormant,

Each beat, a hollow without an echo,

Silent, I await our verse,

The rhythm of a conjoined pulse.

20.

Like vines without a trellis,

My affection winds aimlessly,

Grappling air for structure,

Yearning for the form of you.

21.

The chill of empty sheets,

Cradles a galaxy of unspent warmth,

An unshared blanket, a pillow's hollow—

Each morning, the sun is a harsh reminder,

Of the dawn we've yet to greet, to follow.

This bed—a vessel navigating night's vast sea,

Awaits the captain of its dreams,

To sail into a shared morning's light, serene.

22.

I search the night sky's vastness,

For a star cast in your likeness —

In its flicker, the promise

Of a warmth yet to nestle beside me.

23.

In the hush of evening's tender fold,

A scented petal, free from its floral hold,

Descends like a whisper on to ground's embrace—

The fragrance lingers, a solitary trace.

It carries memories not yet made for sharing,

From blossoms nurtured with silent pairing.

Vivid are hues unseen by your eyes,

Awaiting their witness in patient reprise.

This scent that drifts through quiet air

Speaks softly of moments we've yet to bear.

An aroma promising future delight—

Yet dwelling alone in the gentle night.

Unseen this flower and unshared its sweet breath

Its perfume blooms amidst loneliness' depth.

Silent it stands as time gently flows,

A testament to love that secretly grows.

Now draped in silence where two should have been,

My senses yearn for what is still unseen.

For every drop of dew reflects our story untold;

In each olfactive note, our union could unfold.

The garden lies peaceful under moon's soft glow;

Petals await touch they do not know.

Their essence unfurls without notice or fame —

Till you come forth and call them by name.

24.

Cities teem with a myriad of heartbeats,

Yet mine finds no echo across the deafening pulse.

In the urban orchestra, I am a solo.

Aching for harmony.

25.

Moments are the currency of lovers,

Mine, are coins tossed in a wishing well,

Awaiting the magic that turns them to shared treasures,

Where time is a narrative we've yet to tell.

I hoard each second like gold drachma,

Eager for the transformation,

When time unites and fills fleeting spaces.

26.

In the quiet, I fashion daydreams

Of you, like origami hopes,

Folding corners of reality

Into a delicate wish.

In the silence, I craft visions,

Of you, a tapestry of thought,

Weaving strands of the everyday,

Into a portrait yet uncaught.

In the calm, I sculpt fantasies,

Of you, with the clay of the mundane,

Molding the soft earth of the quotidian,

Into a figure I've yet to name.

In the hush, I compose symphonies,

Of you, notes rising from the lull,

Harmonies spun from the void,

Into a melody beautiful.

27.

Mornings birth aches anew,

Hope stretches, reaching for a sun,

Risen but not awakened,

By the press of your form undone.

28.

Shadows waltz alone in corners,

Yearning for the light to come,

To cut through half-lit hopes,

And dance with a love that's yet to dawn.

29.

In solitude's enduring embrace, I discover

Gentle murmurs of the whispering yet-to-be,

The unsown fields of future's bounty,

Narrating tales of you intertwined with me.

Anticipation is my faithful guest—silent, yet loud,

Its whispers haunting my every move,

Awaiting the arrival of our opening scene,

When life's play commences, and our love proves.

30.

Muted is the solo heart,

Yet within its chambers plays

A melody of future whispers,

A duet destined for brighter days.

31.

The canvas of night stretches wide,

Each star a dot in our unwritten map.

Constellation by constellation,

I trace the path to where our hands might clasp.

32.

In the still canvas stretched wide across night's expanse

Each star punctuates our unwritten story's map.

Constellations await our tracings,

As I plot the course to where our souls might wrap.

I search the celestial byways for a sign,

Of the journey to the warmth of your embrace.

A journey etched in night's own ink,

Guiding me tenderly to your space.

33.

Like a crescendo, these longing builds,

A symphony nearing its peak,

Notes etched in the soul's score,

Building to the moment we finally speak.

The Dawn of Affinity

34.

Whispers turn to laughter,

as surprise finds its echo

in the company of another,

with whom words flow untrodden, free.

Shared smiles, our secret lexicon,

a sotto voce symphony,

Silent understanding, our lore,

a language only we comprehend.

35.

Our hands, like hesitant pilgrims,

Embark upon the journey of touch.

Fingertips tracing stories,

Each contact saying much.

36.

Conversations meander into night,

Two souls cast adrift on shared tides,

Beneath the quiet hum of starlight,

Intimacy in the silence abides.

37.

We bask in newfound warmth,

A sun that rises within the chest.

With every sunset we share,

Promise is laid to rest.

38.

Your gaze, the artist's tender brush,

sweeps across the palette of my days,

Painting hues of ardor upon my skin,

a mural of warmth, of sunlit rays.

With looks that linger longer, soft and hushed,

in eyes I find both dawn and dusk,

Our canvas stretches wide, begins,

to hold the love, we dare entrust.

39.

A whisper of your name,

And suddenly every song is about you,

Melodies wrapped in meaning,

Lyrics aligning as if on cue.

40.

In the hush before dawn's first light,

I watch the calm that graces your face,

Each breath, a gentle anchor in night's embrace,

Our time, a sanctuary, soft and bright.

Whispers of the world asleep, a tender sound,

Underneath the faint, pearlescent glow,

In this quiet, our connected souls resound,

Here, amidst the chaos of life, we find our flow.

41.

Laughter, our shared rhythm, fills the night,

as we step in time to music that sways and dips.

A dance floor all our own, under the lunar light,

reveals where your foot falls, and my missteps.

Hand in hand, we move, finding the feel,

of a partnership in its awkward grace,

In sync we find a tempo real,

that guides us to a tender place.

42.

In the hush of dawn's soft light,

I watch serenity play upon your features,

Each breath you take, a sacred rite,

In our haven of time, our secluded bleachers.

Here, where minutes blend and rush,

Each second swells with life's bright confetti,

In the warm glow of love's first blush,

We find our rhythm, steady and heady.

43.

In your rhythm, I've found my own,

your heartbeat, a beat I now claim.

In your presence, my world has grown.

animated with a spark, a newborn flame.

Your vitality echoes, a call I embrace,

each throb in my chest now a bright enclave

Of joy I nestle in the newfound space,

a treasure trove once stern and grave.

44.

Side by side, our mugs exude warmth,

Their steam ascending in a tender waltz.

Love dwells in these small, shared acts,

Each sip a communion, a moment's grace exalts.

45.

Sunlit threads weave through open blinds,

Catching the dust that dances like our laughter,

Each ray entwines with the day we find,

Our before and ever after.

46.

Our messages, a steady stream,

Flowing into an ocean of inside jokes.

A language birthed from a dream,

Penned in invisible notes.

47.

Your irises hold uncharted lands,

brimming with vistas yet to explore.

Hand in hand, through life's shifting sands,

together, we sail from shore to sure.

The potential of your unfathomable depths,

beckons with each fond gaze,

As across love's oceans and weft,

we chart our joining days.

48.

The whispers of your affection,

Wind through the alleyways of my thoughts.

A gentle, persistent insurrection,

Love carries as it delights and taunts.

49.

Once a solitary figure, now we stand,

Pairing shadows on the ground,

With each step, hand in hand,

A belonging that's profound.

50.

Our burgeoning love takes flight,

Over the landscapes of the ordinary.

Every mundane sight,

Made extraordinary.

51.

The market bustles, but it's you I seek,

in every stall your essence lingers.

The scent of spiced laughter we uniquely speak,

traces of you touched by my fingers.

Blend of conversation, a tapestry, a holy writ,

where your smiles are the currency, I covet in store.

In every interaction, in every wit,

your presence a magnet, a central core.

52.

With each sunrise we greet together,

Morning's glow on familiar sheets,

Love's warmth shelters against any weather,

Our entwined day ahead awaits.

53.

Evening comes, a gentle tide,

Drawing us into the night's embrace.

Side by side, an effortless glide,

In the ebb and flow, our place.

.

Whispers of future whispered back,

A reverberation through shared space.

Together, nothing is what we lack,

In unity, we trace.

55.

Every 'I love you' once lost to the air,

Now finds a home upon your lips,

Every confession I now dare,

into this sacred space it slips.

In you, a haven has been wrought,

from your fidelity, a bastion sought,

Every doubt, once firmly taught,

Unlearns itself, in love's sweet plot.

56.

We walk, your laugh the buoyant air,

Bubbles rising in the light of day.

My heart unfurling from its lair,

Wooed by everything you say.

57.

Coincidence weaves our days,

A pattern emerging from the loom.

In every woven way,

Our affections bloom.

58.

Our confessions spill like morning dew,

Glistening in honesty's early light.

Each reveal, an anchor true,

Holding fast to tender might.

59.

The grammar of our affection, a sanctified text,

Penned in the margins of every endeavor,

Our commitment, subtly, complexly flexed,

a promise etched for the forever.

Your whisper, a clause in love's intricate syntax,

every kiss a sentence, emphatically felt.

In the narrative of us, no need for pretexts,

words become touch, and touch becomes words,

only understood as our hearts melt.

60.

Your name, etched upon my days,

A signature on every hour.

Your love, a labyrinthine maze,

In which I willfully cower.

61.

Nights become a fleet of dreams,

Sailing across the fabric of the dark.

Together, under the moon's beams,

We leave behind an indelible mark.

62.

The world bends in our love's gravity,

An orbit drawn with your smile's arc.

Together redefining sanity,

In every shared remark.

63.

I've grown familiar with the timbre of your words,

Filling the emptiness with vibrant hues.

In the joining of our souls, I find my joy,

Our togetherness, the pinnacle of our times.

64.

Every kiss, a silent covenant,

a quiet vow we configure.

Lips speak in gentle sacrament,

traces of shared future, drawn figure by figure.

In the soft press of moments we compose,

Fleeting touch becomes our composed truth.

A tender inscription, as the hours close,

revealing the poetry of our youth.

65.

Eyes meet, a silent conversation,

Volumes spoken in a glance's span.

In your reflection—my elation,

As love writes a tale that began.

66.

In the cocoon of our embrace,

The world drifts into soft focus,

Lovers in a suspended place,

Bound by emotion's hocus-pocus.

In the Heart's Quiet Bloom.

67.

Love finds a gentle cadence,

in morning coffee rituals,

the silence between us

as comfortable as the soft sweater I wear,

threads woven with the yarn of countless conversations,

warmth not just from the wool but from the familiarity

that has seeped into our bones.

68.

Our conversations unfold beneath the stars,

entwined hands sketching visions of shared tomorrows.

As dusky skies turn to velvet black,

we lay bare the stories of the day just passed,

each revelation adding depth,

to the flourishing garden of our unity.

69.

Your laughter has become my echo,

a resonance that lives in the walls of our home.

Shared sorrows, shared joys,

a harmony invisible, indivisible,

an evolving melody that sings

of two lives merging into one symphony.

70.

Mutual understanding is now our hearth;

fires stoked by trust and tender care.

Comfortable silence our shared berth,

navigating life with a love that's rare.

In this space where emotions ebb and flow,

our bond deepens, undeniably true,

steadfast amidst life's uneven tempo.

71.

In your arms, I've found the strength to be vulnerable,

a safe harbor for my deepest fears.

Our love, now an anchor, unshakable,

the resonance of our commitment clear.

Through seasons of doubt and celestial bright,

we stand united—our love, the lighthouse beam

guiding us through the soft and stormy night.

72.

It's in the gestures unseen,

the cup of tea made just right,

a shared glance across a room,

our own language, our silent commune.

Love is no longer just a flame,

but the ember that glows through both sunshine and rain.

73.

Shared memories are etched upon the soul's mantlepiece,

A collection of snapshots, not of pictures but moments:

The laughter that made our bellies ache,

The book we read aloud on rainy Sundays,

The dance we shared in the kitchen's grace.

74.

Trust is the quiet cornerstone of us,

the unseen foundation holding high the fortress of our union.

Transparency the windows through which we always look,

Truth the door forever open,

And loyalty the roof shielding us from every storm.

75.

We linger in the space between words,

Each pause pregnant with the weight of unsaid love.

An understanding deeper than oceans,

Every silence filled with the sound of our beating hearts.

76.

Time, once the enemy of budding love,

has become an ally in our affection's tale.

No longer measured but cherished,

every second a brushstroke in our shared mural,

every day another shade in our love's palette.

77.

We have found a rhythm in our daily waltz,

Elegance in our repetition,

A sway in our routine.

Comfort in predictability,

Adventure in shared decision,

Each step a silent vow renewed.

78.

Love's once wild storm has settled into

Calm seas of trust and mutual growth.

Where we cherish the quiet after rain,

Find solace in the shared custody of pain.

79.

We trade pieces of our pasts,

like heirlooms unearthed from hidden chests.

You gift me your tales, I bequeath you mine,

In every exchange, our souls further entwine.

80.

With time, love wears smoother,

The sharp edge of infatuation rounded to fit perfectly inside the palm.

Comfort takes the form of a silent nod,

A secret signal known only to us, a sign of our placid calm.

81.

Our love has become a canvas stretched

across the framework of shared years.

Layer upon layer we paint our days,

life's tapestry interwoven with both laughter and tears.

82.

I've navigated the geography of your mind,

travelled the contours of your heart.

Every crevasse familiar, every peak explored,

in the embrace of the soul,

love's map continually unfurled.

83.

Our conversations now have the richness of a vintage wine,

Aged, full-bodied, and shared in quiet celebration.

Every sip, a toast to our complexity,

Our union's continuous maturation.

84.

Shared silence is no longer absence,

but a testament to the depths of our communion.

Where words might once have rushed in

now rests a peaceful understanding,

a love deep like the roots of an ancient tree.

85.

Promises now wear the patina of time,

Yet still they glimmer like tokens newly minted.

In our commitment, the gleam of eternity,

Each assurance, spoken or silent, distinctly printed.

86.

The trust we anchor in each other

Is the bedrock of our daily dawning.

Fears, once looming cliffs,

Now the gravel beneath our conjoined journeying.

87.

Your presence is the note that tunes my morning,

A constancy that draws the melody from the mundane.

My companion in the symphony of daylight,

Our love the refrain that echoes in the refrain.

88.

Comfort has become our shared dialect,

A language crafted in the quiet spaces between us.

Familiarity, a lexicon rich and complex,

Breathing easy in the completeness of trust.

89.

Every shared dream now threaded with the silk of reality,

A tapestry of our joint imaginings coming to life.

In every thread, our reinforced solidity,

Woven tightly in the loom of shared strife

90.

Once effervescent, love's tenure has deepened in taste,

Matured into a vintage that soothes more with each pour.

The once eager rush now savored, no sip made in haste,

Marking time not in moments hurried, but in richness to adore.

91.

Each morning as I trace the contours of your sleeping face,

I find new landscapes, love's gentler pace.

Each expression, a cherished place,

Mapped in the cartography of grace.

92.

In love's quiet vault, we find the treasure

of an affection that has been distilled.

A purity forged in shared pressure,

In mutual space, willingly filled.

93.

Our journey, marked by the rhythm of routine,

Pulses to the beat of shared experience.

In the cadence of the mundane there exists a serene,

The hum of our collective resilience.

94.

We are a composition played in lower keys,

Notes that resonate in the depth of connection.

Music that doesn't need an audience to please,

Harmony that is its own perfect reflection.

95.

Shared sorrow, once a storm,

Now showers to nourish our collective growth.

In our resilience, love finds form,

Binding us beyond the ceremonial oath.

96.

Seasons have turned and so have we,

round each other like celestial bodies in space.

Drawn in an unstoppable gravity,

Circling ever inward, until we align.

97.

In the tapestry of love, we are both weaver and thread,

Intertwining in patterns unforeseen.

With every touch, every word said,

We create a fabric of feeling, vast and serene.

98.

Day by day, our shared life inscribes

a tome of love's thorough script.

A narrative that needs no scribe,

For in our hearts, it's eternally equipped.

99.

Familiar is the laughter that crinkles your eyes,

Love's narrative written in every line.

History shared under ever-shifting skies,

Every glance, a story, every smile, a sign.

Shattered Silhouettes

100.

In the aftermath, the silence after you're gone

sweeps through the once warm corridors of our shared space.

It's a stark, empty canvas where our laughter painted vibrant hues,

a hollow canvas standing still and silent.

Where once the air thrummed

with the life force of our intermingled songs,

there now beats the drum of absence,

a relentless echo in a barren chamber once lush with love's resonance.

101.

Echoes of 'us' ricochet off bare walls —

a ghost dance of memory,

present in its haunting absence.

Each corner, a graveyard of whispers,

our laughter turned to dust.

102.

We sit across a chasm of unsaid words,

the distance between us

a gulf too wide for bridges.

Love fades, a mirage dissolving,

leaving only the thirst of loss.

103.

My hands fumble in the dark,

clutching at the space where yours used to be.

The bed, an expanse of cold emptiness,

grows larger each night,

echoing the vacancy in my chest.

104.

Memories that unfurled like bright sails

are now heavy anchors, submerged in the depths of my mind.

Each remembrance, a sharpened edge; each snapshot, a thorn,

piercing through the fabric of now.

The sweetness of shared moments—once nectar at the lips—

now bitter on the tongue as the heart mourns for a ghost,

an essence vanished, leaving behind only the chill of its shadow,

and the aching light of a sun long set.

105.

Love's melody, now dissonance in the hollows of my mind.

Where euphony once reigned,

cacophony takes root,

and every note we fashioned together

is now a requiem for the departed tune.

106.

Our picture frames now colourless,

the smiles within them faded.

Eyes that once sparkled with shared secrets

now strangers gazing back, jaded.

107.

Promises, once our sacred vows,

lie broken like shards of glass,

scattered on our path.

Barefoot, we tread—each step an echo,

of a covenant that couldn't last.

108.

In the silent gallery of the heart, I roam,

searching for the fissure, the fragile turn

where laughter ceased and silences grew.

Was it a slow fade, a dimming of hearts once ablaze,

or a sudden eclipse, an abrupt nightfall

where love's glow was cruelly extinguished?

The unravelling tapestry, a history I rewind,

in search of the thread that first came loose,

the unravelling of the fabric we once wove with careful hands.

109.

The void engulfs, oceanic and merciless –

it swallows the ship of our journey whole.

No flares or SOS save the remnants,

the depths claim the wreckage of a sunken soul.

110.

The photo albums are a litany of loss,

each page turned, an epitaph for yesterday.

A record of love's archaeology,

sorting relics that time has frayed.

111.

Our garden, once a vivid testament of blossoming promises,

stands neglected—flowers droop, the shrubs untrimmed.

Each bloom that falls, a quiet mourner,

shedding petals like silent tears upon the unforgiving earth.

The vibrancy and colour lost to a hoarfrost of apathy,

each leaf curling in upon itself, as if to shield

from the chill of a gaze turned cold,

reflecting the desolate ground of respect that cracked and faded away.

112.

Questions ricochet through sleepless nights,

searching for the fault lines of our fracture.

Letters, photos, ticket stubs—

every memento now an artifact of rupture.

113.

The pillow bears the weight of sorrow,

a silent testament to the tears spilled.

By dawn, each stain is a map

of the terrain of a heart unfulfilled.

114.

The world, once small within your embrace,

The world, so small and compact within the circle of your arms,

now stretches out, an infinite maze of days and nights unshared.

Places we once filled with our echoes, togetherness echoed in streets and café corners,

looming vast and alien, each corner sharpened into solitary points.

Without the compass of your presence, landscapes morph,

the city's map redrawn—a place where every path, every door,

every sunrise and sunset sing a leaden refrain,

of an overture for one, not two—a lonesome prelude to the days ahead.

115.

In the quiet aftermath —

your departure a silent storm,

I am the aftermath, the echo,

a shell searching for its pearl in the ruin's form.

mending horizons

116.

Tender is the night that shelters a mending heart,

The stars whispering verses of resilience.

Each constellation, a guide back to the start,

A pathway marked with quiet brilliance.

117.

In the subtle grays of early day,

Dawn breaks, whispering promises to the Earth.

There, in the pause between night and morn, find solace—

A gentle reminder that all pain leads toward rebirth.

As light creeps, inch by inch, it softens the edges of grief,

Bathes wounds in warm hues, offering solace, relief.

From each sunrise, draw the courage of forgiveness,

Grasp the hope sewn into the hem of daybreak's garment—

A new beginning stitched with dawn's own thread.

118.

Solitude, once a cold stranger, now comforts,

Teaching the rhythm of self-consoling breaths.

In quiet moments, strength is rediscovered,

A soul relearning its solitary steps.

119.

The laughter that once echoed for two

Finds its way back in solitary echoes.

A chuckle at first, slight and soft,

Slowly blooming into joy's afterglows.

120.

Tears, once daily visitors, come less often,

The moments in between growing clearer,

A softer landscape emerges, less trodden,

Paths to healing drawn nearer.

121.

Reflections in the water, once rippled with disturbances,

Now clear as if stilled by time's gentle hand.

What were ripples of distress have settled into calm,

Showing not the specters of the past, but the shape of what's to stand.

A gaze, steady and true, meets a once-familiar stranger,

Seeing in their own eyes a story yet to write.

In the deep pool of contemplation arises a newfound courage—

A self, reshaped by introspection, molded by the night.

122.

Amidst the ruins of a love once lived, a sprout of self emerges,

A reminder that even in devastation, there is room for new growth.

With each tender unfurling, the heart purges,

Breathing life back into the underbrush.

123.

In the quiet of a room, devoid of another's rhythm,

I have discovered melodies that linger solely in my chest.

Notes that do not mourn for accompaniment,

But revel in the solo that bears their crest.

These refrains, once silence-fearing, now embrace the hush,

With each bar, they pull away from shadows' clutch,

The heart's song, strong in its solitary composing,

Finds a symphony even in solitude, a resonance imposing.

124.

Grains of hope filter through clenched fists,

Seeping into the crevices of a closed heart.

With time, hands open, releasing pasts into mists,

Embracing tomorrow, a canvas reimagined, a new start.

125.

A conversation with the past, an accord with what's lost,

Acknowledgment whispers through the branches.

Beneath the bark, the core still firm, despite the frost,

Enduring through life's avalanches.

126.

In the quiet aftermath, the heart discovers,

A language never lost but forgotten,

Words of self-love written under the covers,

Of a bed that's no longer downtrodden.

127.

The line where Earth kisses sky, once a limit, now extends a call—

To witness daybreak, paint its aspirations for tomorrow.

Each stroke a shade of potential, a hand to lead one through the sorrow,

Sunrise, a masterful artist, conceals the last night's pall.

So let your gaze follow were morning paints anew,

Allow each dawn to colour your canvas with a hopeful view,

In the skies, ever shifting, find a path through the azure venue,

Promising a journey unweighted, a spirit unscrewed.

128.

Where there was you, now there is me,

A rediscovery of space in my own beat,

A dance of one, with light steps and free,

A solo performance, nonetheless, complete.

129.

Like the moon's sure cycle, hearts too, renew,

Resurfacing from the dark, into the light.

A gentle pull toward the next phase's view,

Guided by internal gravity, by innate might.

130.

Even after the inferno, when you feel the earth must surely be barren,

Nature reveals her fortitude, her green shoots defiant in charred ground.

Our hearts, akin to these seeds, reach for the sun despite the dark's summons,

Roots penetrate with intrinsic desire to grow, and to abound.

Through the ashen layers of past fires, through the pain and all preceding liars,

Sprouts the verdant proof of inner strength and will,

A testament to life's resolve, even in the face of desolate biers,

Showing nothing can silence the heart's relentless quill.